Walt Disney's
Surprise for Mickey Mouse

A GOLDEN BOOK, New York
Western Publishing Company, Inc.
Racine, Wisconsin 53404

GOLDEN, A LITTLE GOLDEN BOOK®, and GOLDEN PRESS®
are trademarks of Western Publishing Company, Inc.

"Uncle Mickey!" shouted Morty Mouse. "Look!"
"Here's a telegram for you!" cried Ferdie.
"Huh?" said Mickey Mouse. He sat up in his
hammock. "A telegram? What could it be?"
"I know a keen way to find out," said Morty.
"Open it."

So Mickey opened the telegram.

"Is it good news?" asked Ferdie.

"It's great news!" cried Mickey. "Walt Disney World is going to have a Mickey Mouse Revue. And guess who's going to direct the orchestra!"

"You are!" laughed Mickey's nephews.
"That's right!" said Mickey proudly.
"I'll press your dress suit," said Morty.
"And I'll get the airplane tickets," said Ferdie.

"And I'll run and tell Minnie," said Mickey. "She'll be so thrilled."

But Minnie did not seem at all thrilled by Mickey's good news. "That's nice," she said, "but I can't stop to chat. I'm going downtown to buy a new hat."

Mickey was very disappointed. But just then Horace Horsecollar wandered along.

"Horace!" said Mickey. "Guess what! I'm going to lead the orchestra at Walt Disney World."

"You are?" said Horace. "Well, that's fine, if you like that sort of thing."

Mickey hurried on till he met the Three Little Pigs. "Did you hear?" said Mickey. "I'm going to lead the orchestra at Walt Disney World."

"Good luck," said Practical Pig calmly. "And don't touch my new wall. The mortar's still wet."

"Geppetto and Pinocchio will be glad to hear about my musical revue," said Mickey to himself.

But at Geppetto's shop, the old wood-carver was so busy painting faces on dolls that he couldn't even stop to listen.

As for Pinocchio, he was fishing Figaro the kitten out of Cleo's goldfish bowl. "What's an orchestra?" asked Pinocchio.

"Never mind," said Mickey sadly. "If you don't know, I won't try to explain it."

Mickey hurried to Donald Duck's house. Donald
and his nephews, Huey, Dewey, and Louie, were
playing baseball in the backyard.

"Know what happened to me?" called Mickey.

"What?" asked Donald. "Don't tell me Pluto took first prize at the dog show."

"No," said Mickey. "I'm going to have my own musical revue at Walt Disney World."

"Oh, that!" said Donald Duck.
"Big deal!" said Huey, Dewey, and Louie.
And they went back to their baseball game.

Mickey walked on, feeling terribly forlorn, until he came to the circus at the edge of town. There was Dumbo the elephant, with his friend Timothy the mouse.

"Hi!" called Mickey. "Know what? I'm going to lead the orchestra at Walt Disney World."

"That's nice," said Timothy. "Have fun."

"Want to see me fly?" asked Dumbo, and he spread his big ears and soared off.

"Doesn't Dumbo fly beautifully?" said a voice at Mickey's elbow. It was Daisy Duck.

"Yes," snapped Mickey. "For an elephant, he flies very well. But did you know that I'm going to Walt Disney World to lead the orchestra?"

"That will be lovely," said Daisy. "Not as lovely as flying, of course, but rather nice."

"Oh, never mind!" shouted Mickey, and he stomped away.

When Mickey got home, he found that his
nephews had the suitcases packed, and they had the
airplane tickets.

"We're all going," laughed Ferdie. "Even Pluto.
We wouldn't miss it for anything!"

"I'm glad," said Mickey. "No one else cares!"

And the next day, on the plane, Mickey brooded
all the way to Florida.

But when the plane landed and Mickey saw Walt Disney World, he began to cheer up. It was such a friendly place, and everyone he saw was having a wonderful time.

"There's a sign over there," said Morty. "It says, 'Mickey Mouse Revue.' "

"That's your theater!" said Ferdie.

"Fine," said Mickey. "Let's go and meet the members of the orchestra."

Mickey hurried into the theater to meet the orchestra. "Oh, my!" he said.

For there were Donald and Daisy, and Huey, Dewey, and Louie. There were Minnie Mouse and Horace Horsecollar and the Three Little Pigs. There were Geppetto and Pinocchio and Dumbo and Timothy and . . . well, all of Mickey's friends.

"Surprise!" they cried. "We're your orchestra!"

"And you thought we didn't care!" said Minnie Mouse.

Mickey had never been so happy. His musical revue was wonderful. The audience clapped and cheered, and Mickey's orchestra took twenty-seven bows.

They would have taken twenty-eight, but Donald Duck got so excited that he fell into a bass drum.